# The
# Puppy Problem

"Hey—here's a crumb!" Nancy cried, pointing at the sidewalk. "Maybe it's a clue."

"Where?" Bess asked. Holding the puppy's leash, she ran down the driveway to see.

Just then the puppy pulled hard on the leash. She broke free from Bess and ran to Nancy. Instantly, she sniffed the ground and licked the crumb.

"She ate the clue!" George cried.

"Bess, you have to hold on to her," Nancy scolded.

But it was too late. The puppy darted between Nancy's legs and scampered away!

# The Nancy Drew Notebooks

Available from Simon & Schuster

# THE
# NANCY DREW
# NOTEBOOKS®

#12

*The Puppy Problem*

## CAROLYN KEENE
ILLUSTRATED BY ANTHONY ACCARDO

**Aladdin Paperbacks**
New York  London  Toronto  Sydney  Singapore

First Aladdin Paperbacks edition April 2002
First Minstrel Books edition May 1996
Copyright © 2005 by Simon & Schuster, Inc

ALADDIN PAPERBACKS
An imprint of Simon & Schuster
Children's Publishing Division
1230 Avenue of the Americas
New York, NY 10020

The text of this book was set in Excelsior.

Printed in the United States of America.
10

ISBN 0-671-53551-X (ISBN-13: 978-0-671-53551-3)

# The Puppy Problem

# 1

# The New Puppy

Look, Daddy. It's licking my face!" Nancy Drew cried.

Eight-year-old Nancy was cuddling a puppy in her arms. She let it sniff her reddish blond hair.

At her feet, three other puppies scampered and played in the grass.

"Hold her under her tummy," Mr. Brachman said.

Mr. Brachman owned a kennel and raised Labrador retrievers. His dog Molly was the puppies' mother.

"I'm *trying* to hold her," Nancy said, giggling. "But she wiggles!"

Just then the puppy licked Nancy—right on the nose! Nancy laughed. "I want this one."

"She does seem to like you," Mr. Brachman said. He laughed, too. "She's the puppy I had in mind for you."

"How old are the puppies?" Nancy's father asked.

"They're ten weeks old," Mr. Brachman answered. "Just the right age to be adopted. The vet checked them yesterday and gave them their first shots."

"Shots?" Nancy asked. She made a face. "I don't like shots. Did the puppies cry?"

"No," Mr. Brachman said. "Puppies don't mind too much. And they need their shots so they won't get sick."

Mr. Drew paid Mr. Brachman. Then Mr. Brachman told Nancy how to take care of her new puppy.

"Now, remember," Mr. Brachman said. "Labs are smart and easy to train. But you have to start early. She's going to grow up to be a big dog. Be nice, but be firm with her."

"We will," Nancy promised. She and

her father put the puppy in a large wire dog crate in the back of their car for the ride home.

"Are you sure she'll be okay in there?" Nancy asked, frowning.

"Yes," Carson Drew said. "And remember, Mr. Brachman told us we have to get her used to the crate right away so she'll know it's her home."

Nancy nodded. The puppy curled up on the blanket on the floor of the crate and looked at Nancy with big, friendly brown eyes.

Nancy had asked her father for a dog every single day for a long time. Finally he'd said, "Maybe." Then he and Nancy talked about what kind of dog to get. They decided on a Labrador retriever because Labs were such nice, friendly dogs.

When Nancy's father pulled into the driveway, Bess Marvin and her cousin George Fayne were waiting. They were Nancy's best friends.

Bess's blond hair flew behind her as she ran toward the car. But George ran

3

faster. Her long legs pumped hard. Her short dark curls bounced up and down.

"Did you get a dog?" George called.

"Yes!" Nancy said. She jumped out of the car and took out her puppy.

"Oh, look! How cute!" Bess cried.

"It's brown?" George asked, sounding surprised. "I thought Labrador retrievers were black."

"Not always," Nancy said. "Sometimes they're yellow. Or brown, like my puppy. She's a *chocolate* Lab."

"I have to go into the office for a while," Mr. Drew said to Nancy. "But I'll put the crate in the room off the kitchen. Hannah will help you get the puppy settled."

Nancy nodded.

"Come on. Let's take her into the backyard to play," Bess said. "It's fenced in so she'll be safe and can't run away."

All three girls hurried to the backyard to let the puppy run free. It was fun to watch her. They sat in the grass and let the puppy climb all over them.

"I smell something yummy," Bess said suddenly. She stood up and hurried to the gate.

Bess opened the gate and walked down the driveway toward the kitchen door. The door was on the side of the house facing the driveway.

Nancy and George and the puppy jumped up and followed Bess.

"Look—chocolate chip muffins!" Bess said happily. She pointed through the screen door at a dozen freshly baked muffins sitting on a bench just inside the kitchen door.

"Can we have one?" George asked as she pushed the door open.

"No, girls," a woman's voice answered. "It's too close to dinner."

Hannah Gruen came into the kitchen. Hannah had been the Drew family's housekeeper for five years, ever since Nancy's mother died.

"Oh, *please*, Hannah," Bess said. "They smell so good."

Hannah laughed and shook her head.

"Nope. Sorry," she said. "They're for dinner tonight."

Just then the puppy scrambled across the kitchen floor toward Hannah's feet.

"Oh!" Hannah cried. "How cute!" She bent down to let the puppy lick her hand. "Your father put her crate in the little room off the kitchen," she told Nancy.

"Maybe when she's a little older—and after she's housebroken—she can sleep with me," Nancy said.

Hannah wrinkled her nose. "I don't know about that," she said. "But just remember our deal. You have to take care of her—feed her, walk her, brush her. It's a big job."

"I remember," Nancy said. "I'll keep my promise."

Nancy, Bess, and George took the puppy and went back outside. When they reached the back gate, they saw a sandy-haired, freckle-faced boy standing there.

"What's *he* doing here?" Bess said in a snippy voice.

"Shhh," Nancy said. The boy was Kenny Bruder. He lived in Nancy's neighborhood. He was in the fourth grade—a year ahead of Nancy and her friends.

"You got a dog," Kenny said to Nancy. Nancy thought he sounded both jealous and sad. "Can I pet him?"

"Sure," Nancy said. "But it's not a him. It's a her."

"I wish I had a dog," Kenny said. "More than anything."

"Why don't you get a dog, if you want one so much?" George asked.

"My mom won't let me," Kenny said. He petted the puppy some more. "What kind of dog is this, anyway?"

"A chocolate Lab," Nancy answered.

"Chocolate?" Kenny said. "Weird. I'm allergic to chocolate." He stood up. "Can I teach her some tricks?"

"Not now," Bess said before Nancy could answer. "*We* want to play with her first. Nancy just got her."

"And anyway she's too young to learn tricks," Nancy said. "Come back

in a few days," she added, trying to be nice. "I'll let you play with her after she gets used to us."

"Yeah. Come back some other time," Bess said, wrinkling her nose.

George nudged her cousin in the side. "Be nice," George whispered.

"No way," Bess said as Kenny walked slowly away. "He's a boy."

Nancy rolled her eyes. Then she turned. "Now where's my puppy?" she asked. Suddenly the puppy came running toward her from under the kitchen steps.

Nancy and her friends took the puppy into the backyard. For the next half hour, Nancy, Bess, and George played with the puppy. They let her chew on a stick. They let her run around in circles.

Then Nancy let the puppy lie in her lap when she was all tired out.

"Nancy!" a voice suddenly called sharply from the driveway.

Nancy looked up and saw Hannah standing there with her hands on her hips. She had a scowl on her face. "Did you girls eat those muffins?" Hannah asked.

"No," Nancy said, shaking her head fast.

"Now, tell the truth," Hannah said, still sounding angry.

"No, really," Bess said. "We didn't."

"Well, if you didn't eat them, who did?" Hannah asked. "Because three muffins are gone!"

# 2

# Missing Muffins

**N**ancy felt her face turn red. Was Hannah really accusing her of stealing food?

"We *didn't* take them," Nancy protested. Her voice almost squeaked.

Hannah said, "Well, *someone* took them. And I wouldn't be surprised if it was that puppy of yours."

"No," Nancy said firmly. "She was with us the whole time."

"But she escaped once and hid under the steps," Bess said. "Remember?"

"See?" Hannah said. "She probably

pushed the door open and ate those muffins and the paper cups, too!"

"No!" Nancy cried again.

"You have to watch puppies *every* minute," Hannah scolded gently. "Now she'll probably be sick. I should have told you—chocolate isn't good for dogs. Not even for chocolate Labs." Hannah hurried back into the house.

Nancy smiled slightly at Hannah's joke. But she still felt upset. First Hannah had accused Nancy and her friends of stealing. Then she'd accused Nancy's new dog!

"We *have* to find out who took Hannah's muffins," Nancy said.

"A mystery!" Bess exclaimed. "Super!"

"Come on," Nancy said. "Let's go look for clues."

Nancy clipped a new red leash to the puppy's new red collar. Then she and the puppy hurried down the driveway toward the kitchen door. George and Bess followed. Suddenly Nancy stopped at the screen door.

"What? What's wrong? Are more muffins missing?" Bess asked.

"No," Nancy said. She pointed. "But look. There's a clue."

Nancy handed the puppy's leash to Bess. Then she bent down to take a closer look. Something was caught on the edge of the screen door.

"What is it?" George asked, crowding in closer to see.

"It's a piece of a shoelace," Nancy said. She pulled the clue from the door frame and held it up.

The piece of shoelace had black and white stripes. It was dirty and tattered and about six inches long.

"Hmmm," Nancy said. "It might be from the thief's shoe."

"How do you know?" Bess asked.

"Because I don't have any shoes with laces like that. Neither does Hannah. And neither does Daddy," Nancy said.

"How about Kenny? Maybe it's from his shoe," George said. "Maybe *he* took the muffins."

"Maybe," Nancy said. "But I don't

think so. Remember? He told us he's allergic to chocolate. So I don't think he took the muffins."

Nancy looked around the kitchen quickly. But there were no more clues. Then she hurried outside.

"Let's look for crumbs," Nancy said. "Maybe whoever took the muffins ate them as they ran away. Maybe they left a trail—like Hansel and Gretel."

"You're so smart," Bess said, admiringly. "No wonder you're a great detective."

Nancy grinned and headed down the driveway. She loved looking for clues and solving mysteries.

"Hey—here's a crumb!" Nancy cried, pointing at the sidewalk.

"Where?" Bess asked. Holding the puppy's leash, she ran down the driveway to see.

Just then the puppy pulled hard on the leash. She broke free from Bess and ran to Nancy. Instantly, the puppy sniffed the ground and licked the crumb.

"She ate the clue!" George cried.

"Bess, you have to hold on to her," Nancy scolded.

But it was too late. The puppy darted between Nancy's legs and scampered away!

# 3

# Puppy on the Loose

Come back!" Nancy cried. She chased after her puppy.

But the puppy ran to the end of the block and disappeared.

"Here, puppy!" Nancy called, running after the puppy. "Here, girl!"

George and Bess raced after Nancy. They stopped at the end of the block. The puppy was gone!

"Did you see where she went?" Bess asked, out of breath.

"No," Nancy said. "She disappeared."

"I'm so sorry," Bess said. "I didn't know I had to hold on so tight."

Nancy bit her lip. What if her puppy ran away and never came back? A lump started to form in her throat.

Suddenly something rustled in the bushes beside the three girls.

All at once the puppy dashed out from the hedge.

Instantly Nancy grabbed for the leash. But before she could get it, the puppy turned the corner and dashed away again.

"Wait! Come back!" Nancy called as she ran to catch up.

Bess and George ran, too. They followed the puppy all the way to the Ratazcheks' front yard. Mrs. Ratazchek was kneeling at a flower bed in front of her house. Her pink- and yellow-flowered blouse matched the colors of the flowers in her garden.

"Whoa! What's this?" Mrs. Ratazchek said when the puppy ran up to her and started jumping on her.

"Hold her! That's my dog!" Nancy yelled.

Quickly Mrs. Ratazchek grabbed the

leash. Nancy ran up and took it. She held the leash tight.

"Don't do that," Nancy scolded the puppy gently. "Don't run away like that!"

"Hello, Nancy," Mrs. Ratazchek said, smiling up at her. "Nice to see you. Did you get a new dog?"

"Yes," Nancy said. "And she's getting into all kinds of trouble already."

"Puppies do that," Mrs. Ratazchek said with a smile. "What kind of trouble?"

Nancy told Mrs. Ratazchek about the missing muffins—and how Hannah had blamed it on the dog.

"Missing muffins? Hmmm," Mrs. Ratazchek said. "You know, I've had trouble with some missing food, too," she told Nancy.

"Really? When?" Nancy asked.

"Yesterday," Mrs. Ratazchek said. "Someone stole some groceries right out of the trunk of my car."

"Weird," George said. "What happened?"

"Well, I had five bags of groceries," Mrs. Ratazchek explained. "While I was carrying the fourth bag into the house, I got a phone call. I was on the phone for about five minutes. When I got back outside, guess what? The last bag of groceries was gone!"

"Wow," Bess said. "It's like there's a food thief on the loose."

"I hate to say it, but I think I know who took the food," Mrs. Ratazchek said.

"Who?" Nancy asked eagerly.

Mrs. Ratazchek bit her lip. She looked as if she didn't want to gossip— and didn't want to say something that might not be true.

"Ralph Caruso, a man who does some yard work for me," Mrs. Ratazchek finally answered.

"Oh, I know him," Nancy said. "He's a handyman who works for a lot of people around here. He's worked for us a few times, too."

"Yes," Mrs. Ratazchek said. "Ralph has always been very nice and trustworthy.

But he recently lost his regular job in a hardware store. I don't think he has much money. He might have been hungry."

"But did you see him anywhere around here yesterday?" Nancy asked.

"Oh, yes. He was working for me, mowing the lawn. He finished up and left just as I got home from the grocery store," Mrs. Ratazchek said.

"Hmmm," Nancy said. "Did you see anyone else around at the same time?"

Mrs. Ratazchek scratched her head for a minute and thought. "Well . . . yes," she said finally. "There was that boy. That teenager Sam McCorry."

"Laura's brother?" Bess asked with interest. Laura was a third-grader. But she was not in Nancy, Bess, and George's class at school.

"Yes," Mrs. Ratazchek said. "He was skating in the street when I was unloading the food."

"He's huge," Bess said to Nancy. "Remember? He's a football player."

Nancy thought about Sam for a minute. He *was* big, and Laura always talked about how much he ate. Maybe he was skating around the neighborhood, stealing people's food.

"I wonder what color the laces on his skates are," Nancy said out loud.

"I didn't notice," Mrs. Ratazchek said. "But that reminds me of something else I noticed yesterday."

"What?" Nancy asked.

"Paw prints," Mrs. Ratazchek said. "When Ralph finished mowing the lawn, he turned the sprinkler on. So the grass was wet. I saw wet dog prints on the driveway, right by my car."

"Well, it wasn't Nancy's dog," Bess said quickly. "Nancy didn't even have a dog then."

"Oh, I know that," Mrs. Ratazchek said with a laugh.

Hmmm, Nancy thought. The paw prints might be a clue. She could hardly wait to go home and write it all down in her special detective's notebook.

They all said good-bye to Mrs. Ratazchek. Then Nancy said good-bye to

George and Bess, because it was time for them to go home.

Holding the leash tightly, Nancy walked her puppy home.

Suddenly a large tan dog ran out from behind a tree. The dog was dirty and didn't have a collar on, and it looked kind of lost. Nancy recognized the dog right away. She had seen him running loose in the neighborhood before.

Nancy's puppy pulled on her leash, trying to get closer to the stray. But Nancy wouldn't let her.

"No, you don't. No playing with other dogs," Nancy said. "Not until you have all of your shots."

As Nancy watched the big stray cross the street, she got an idea.

"Hey, wait a minute," Nancy called.

The big stray dog ignored her.

I wonder, Nancy thought. Could that be the dog that left paw prints near Mrs. Ratazchek's car? Was he the food thief?

No way, Nancy decided. How could a dog carry away a big bag of groceries?

Nancy hurried home and put her puppy in the backyard.

"Stay here," she told her puppy. "I'll be right back."

Then she raced into the house and went up to her room. She took her special blue notebook from her desk. With a pen in one hand and the notebook in the other, she hurried back downstairs to her puppy.

But as she pushed through the screen door, Nancy gasped.

There was Ralph Caruso, standing by the back gate. And he had her puppy in his arms!

# 4

# Let Go of My Dog!

**N**ancy's heart started to pound. What was Ralph Caruso doing with her puppy?

She ran up to the burly older man and grabbed his arm.

"Let go of my dog!" she cried. "Put her down!"

"I'm not hurting her," Ralph Caruso said in his deep, gravelly voice. "I just want to look at her."

With his thick, muscular hand, Ralph gently scratched the puppy on her neck. Then he set her down in the grass and let her run free.

"She's a cute one," he said, smiling at Nancy.

"What are you doing here?" Nancy asked.

"I'm doing some yard work for your father," Ralph explained. "Mrs. Gruen went to get me a garden hose from the garage."

Nancy carefully watched Ralph's face. He didn't look as though he was lying. But she was still suspicious. First Ralph was at Mrs. Ratazchek's house when her food was stolen. Now he was at Nancy's house on the same day that the muffins were missing!

Quickly Nancy glanced down at Ralph's shoes—and his shoelaces. The laces were brown, *not* black- and white-striped. They didn't match the clue she had found in the kitchen door.

"Sorry if I scared you," Ralph said.

"That's okay," Nancy said. "I was just surprised."

With the puppy at her heels, Nancy walked across the yard and sat down under a tree. She opened her special blue notebook and turned to a clean page.

At the top, she wrote, "The Case of the Missing Muffins."

Under that, she wrote:

Suspects:
Ralph Caruso, Sam McCorry,
Kenny Bruder.

Then she wrote:

Clue #1: Broken black-and-white shoelace.
Clue #2: Crumbs—eaten by my new puppy!
Clue #3: Wet dog footprints near Mrs. Ratazchek's car.
Ralph's shoelaces—brown.
Kenny—allergic to chocolate.
Sam—eats *a lot!*

Nancy tried to think about all the suspects and clues. But the puppy wouldn't let her. She kept climbing on Nancy's lap and licking Nancy's ear.

"Down, puppy," Nancy said.

Just then Hannah called from the gate. "What are you going to name her?"

"I don't know yet," Nancy said.

Nancy tore a sheet of paper from her notebook. She made a list of all the names she had thought of.

Bess liked the names Princess and Lady.

George had come up with Scamp and Scout. She had also thought of Fudge, since the puppy was a chocolate Lab.

Nancy had thought up her own names for a chocolate Lab. Her favorite was Cocoa.

But none of the names sounded just right.

"How about Muffin?" Hannah said with a twinkle in her eye.

Nancy shook her head hard. "She *didn't* steal your muffins!" Nancy said.

"Maybe . . . and maybe not," Hannah teased. "But if the puppy didn't eat them, who did?"

*       *       *

I need proof, Nancy thought.

That was the second thing she thought when she woke up the next morning. The *first* thing she thought about was her new puppy. Nancy could hardly wait to see her and play with her again.

Nancy hopped out of bed and ran downstairs. It was Saturday—the puppy's first full day at home.

"Good morning, Pudding Pie," Nancy's father said as Nancy dashed into the kitchen.

"Hi, Daddy," Nancy said.

She hurried into the small room off the kitchen. Nancy unlatched the door of the crate. The puppy jumped up from the blanket. She wagged her tail and came running out of the crate.

Nancy gave the puppy a fresh bowl of water and some food. Then she knelt down to play with her on the floor.

"Have you decided on a name yet?" Carson Drew asked.

"Not yet," Nancy said as the puppy tried to bite the belt of her bathrobe.

"How about Pudding Pie Two? You could name her after yourself," Carson Drew said.

"Don't be silly," Nancy said. "My name's not Pudding Pie. That's just your nickname for me."

Just then the puppy pulled hard on Nancy's bathrobe belt.

"Look! She wants to go to the park," Nancy said. "So do I."

"You can go to the park after breakfast," Carson answered. "But the puppy can't. She has to wait until she has all of her shots before she can play with other dogs."

After breakfast Nancy put on a pair of blue jeans and tennis shoes and a red T-shirt. Then she put her puppy in the fenced backyard, so it could run around while she was gone.

When Nancy reached the park, she skipped through the grass, picking dandelions as she went. Then she ran the rest of the way to the swings.

She had just started to swing when

she saw someone—someone who looked like Sam McCorry.

He was skating near the picnic tables.

Nancy hopped off the swing and hurried across the park toward the picnic area.

As she got closer, Nancy saw that a large family had spread out all their food on two tables. But they weren't eating yet. They were playing Frisbee.

Just then Sam skated up to one of the picnic tables. In a flash, he grabbed a cookie from a plate. Nancy's mouth fell open. It was a chocolate chip cookie.

Then he skated away as fast as he could!

# 5

# Chocolate Chips, Gone Again!

Stop! Come back!" Nancy shouted.

But Sam kept right on skating.

Nancy ran after him. Sam glanced over his shoulder at Nancy. She saw a sneaky smile on his face.

Then he popped the whole chocolate chip cookie in his mouth and zoomed out of the park. In an instant he was completely out of Nancy's sight.

"What a creep!" Nancy said out loud.

Nancy glanced back toward the picnic tables. The family had gone back to playing Frisbee. They didn't seem to care that one of their cookies had been stolen.

Nancy decided to go home. As she walked, she heard a scratching sound on the sidewalk. Nancy turned and saw the tan stray dog trotting along behind her. It seemed to be following her.

"No, no," Nancy said. "Go away. You can't come home with me. I already have a puppy."

As soon as she spoke to him, the big stray trotted up to Nancy and sniffed her hand.

"Stay," Nancy said firmly. She pointed to the dog and said it again. "Stay."

Then she crossed the street. She looked behind her. The stray was still sitting on the opposite sidewalk. He seemed to know what "stay" meant.

Too bad that dog doesn't have a home, Nancy thought. He seemed like a nice dog, even if he was scruffy looking.

All of a sudden, a deep, gravelly voice startled her. "Hi, again," it said.

"What?" Nancy said. She looked all around. But she couldn't see anyone!

"Down here," the voice said.

Nancy looked down and saw Ralph Caruso kneeling in the bushes in a neighbor's yard. He was wearing thick leather gloves and was digging a hole.

"Oh, hi," Nancy said, stepping back. "You scared me. What are you doing— burying something?"

"No," Ralph said with a laugh. "I'm trying to dig out these weeds for Dave Tang. He hired me to do some yard work. But the weeds are stubborn. They don't want to come out."

Hmmm, Nancy thought as she walked on. This was a very strange day. First she ran into Sam McCorry. Then the stray dog started following her. And now Ralph Caruso seemed to be there every time she turned around.

It's almost as if my suspects are following *me*, Nancy thought.

When she reached her driveway, Nancy skipped all the way to the backyard.

"Hi, puppy," Nancy called. Instantly, the puppy came running.

Nancy picked her up and cuddled her in her arms. Then she carried her into the house. As soon as she walked in, Nancy noticed that the kitchen smelled good. Hannah was bending over the oven, pulling out a pan of chocolate chip muffins.

"Mmmm—muffins!" Nancy said.

"Yes, and don't let your dog eat them this time," Hannah scolded in a friendly voice.

"She didn't eat them *last* time," Nancy protested.

"Maybe," Hannah said. "Maybe not."

"No fair," Nancy said. She rubbed noses with the puppy and kissed it on the head. "Don't listen to Hannah," Nancy said. "She doesn't know what she's talking about."

But just to be sure, Nancy carried her puppy back outside, far away from the muffins. She didn't want to take a chance that the puppy might eat one *this* time. Then Hannah would never stop teasing her about it. And worse, what if the chocolate made her puppy sick?

For the rest of the day, Nancy played with the puppy. She brushed her, took her for a walk, and played fetch with her.

"How's it going?" Carson Drew called from the back gate as Nancy threw a stick for her puppy to chase.

"Great!" Nancy said. "She seems to know how to fetch things. I didn't even have to teach her."

Nancy's dad laughed. "That's because she's a Labrador retriever," he said. "All retrievers will fetch. *Retrieve* means to go get something and bring it back."

"That's so cool," Nancy said.

"I think so, too," Carson said with a smile.

After dinner Nancy and her father took the dog for another walk. They walked around two blocks, right past the house where Nancy had seen Ralph Caruso digging weeds.

"Daddy, do you trust Ralph Caruso?" Nancy asked.

"Sure," her father said. "Why do you ask?"

"Because he's always around when food is stolen," Nancy said.

She told her father about the groceries that were stolen from Mrs. Ratazchek's car. And about how Ralph Caruso had been at the Drews' house right after the muffins were taken.

"Oh, that doesn't mean anything," her father said.

"I know, but—" Nancy started to say.

But just then she heard a noise coming from behind Dave Tang's house.

Nancy froze. A chill ran down her back. Then she heard the noise again.

"What's that?" Nancy said.

"I don't know," Carson Drew said. "It sounded like a scream!"

# 6

# The Burger Burglar

That scream came from Dave Tang's backyard," Carson Drew said. He and Nancy rushed toward the gate in back.

"Hello, Dave?" Carson called. "Everything okay?"

Dave Tang looked up and waved with the spatula he had in his hand.

Then he walked over to the gate to talk to Nancy and her dad.

"Hi, Carson. Hi, Nancy," Dave said. "You won't believe this, but someone just stole four hamburgers—right off my picnic table!"

"Really?" Nancy said. Her eyes lit up.

She couldn't believe it. More food was missing—and right on her block, too.

"What happened?" Nancy's father asked.

"I was cooking hamburgers on the grill," Dave said. "I put four of them on a plate and set it on the picnic table. Then I went into the house to get the salad. When I came outside again, they were gone."

"Probably some stray dog ate them," Carson said.

"No way," Dave said. He pointed with his spatula. "I've got a fence around the whole yard. And the gate was closed. A dog couldn't get in here."

"What about Ralph Caruso?" Nancy said.

"What about him?" Dave asked.

"Well, I saw him here earlier today. I thought maybe he stole the food," Nancy said. But she blushed when she said it. It felt strange to accuse someone of stealing when she didn't have any proof.

"I don't think so," Dave said, shaking his head. "Ralph's very trustworthy. Besides, he went home on the bus hours ago."

Nancy's father laughed and shook his head. "Well, it sure is a mystery." he said. "And you know my daughter—she loves a good mystery. I wouldn't be surprised if she had it solved by tomorrow."

Dave smiled. "That'll be a little too late," he said. "We want dinner tonight."

All the way home Nancy was quiet. She was thinking hard about the missing burgers.

"I know!" Nancy said, just as she and her father reached their house.

"What?" her father asked.

"The house *behind* Dave's," Nancy said. "That's where Laura McCorry lives."

"So? You think Laura stole the hamburgers?" Carson asked with a twinkle in his eye.

"No," Nancy said. "I think her big

brother, Sam, did. Let's go back to see if Sam is home."

"Not now," Carson said. "It's too late. You'll have to do your detective work tomorrow."

Nancy could hardly wait to get out of the house the next morning. She jumped out of bed and ate breakfast quickly. Then she got dressed.

But before she left the house, she opened her detective's notebook. She made a list of all the reasons why Sam McCorry was her best suspect.

Nancy wrote:

1. He was seen outside Mrs. R's house the day the groceries were stolen.

2. He stole a chocolate chip cookie, which proves he likes chocolate chips. (Did he steal chocolate chip muffins, too?)

3. His house is right behind Dave

Tang's house, where the
burgers were stolen.

4.

Nancy couldn't think of anything for
number 4, so she left it blank.

After that, she hurried downstairs
and attached the red leash to her puppy's red collar.

"Where are you going so early?"
Hannah asked as Nancy and the puppy
headed toward the kitchen door.

"To Laura McCorry's house," Nancy
said. "I'm still trying to solve the case
of the missing muffins. Only now it's
three muffins, a bag of groceries, and
four hamburgers hot off the grill—and
a chocolate chip cookie."

"Oh," Hannah said. "Well, maybe
your puppy isn't the thief after all."

"Of course not," Nancy said. "She
couldn't steal all that food."

"I know," Hannah said. "Maybe I
shouldn't have accused her. I guess I

was just a little nervous about having a new pet in the house."

"That's okay," Nancy said. Then she hurried toward the door.

She led her puppy outside. Outdoors in the sunshine and fresh air, the puppy jumped up with excitement. She wagged her tail and licked Nancy's leg.

Nancy giggled. It was so much fun having a dog!

When Nancy got to Laura's house, she stood on the sidewalk for a moment.

Then she ducked down low and crept up the driveway to the McCorrys' backyard.

I wonder how easy it is to climb over the fence into the Tangs' backyard, Nancy thought.

"Hey, what are *you* doing here?" a voice behind Nancy said.

Nancy jumped. Her dog barked. Laura McCorry was standing behind them on the back patio.

"Oh, uh, hi," Nancy said.

"What are you doing in our back-yard?" Laura repeated.

Nancy's face turned red. She thought for a minute. Could she come up with a good reason for snooping around?

Oh, well, Nancy decided. She might as well tell Laura the truth.

Quickly she explained about the food thief. And about the shoelace. And how she had seen Sam steal a chocolate chip cookie in the park.

"So I wanted to spy on your brother," Nancy admitted. "I wanted to see if any of his shoes or skates have black-and-white laces in them."

Laura narrowed her eyes. "Really? Is that what you're doing here?" she asked.

"Yes," Nancy said.

"Great!" Laura said, clapping her hands together. "I'll help you. It sounds like fun!"

Nancy giggled.

"Come on," Laura said. "Sam's not home. We can sneak up to his room."

"But what about my dog?" Nancy asked.

"Oh, you can tie her up out here on the back patio," Laura said.

Nancy gave her puppy a quick hug. "Be good," she said.

Then she quickly tied the leash around the leg of a lounge chair. She and Laura hurried into the house. Quietly they crept up the stairs to the second floor. Sam's room was at the end of the hall.

"Hold your nose," Laura said. "His room is gross. He never washes his clothes."

Nancy didn't hold her nose. But she did hold her breath. She felt kind of scared, sneaking into someone else's room.

"See what I mean?" Laura said as she swung open Sam's door.

Nancy nodded and gulped. There were T-shirts and socks all over the floor. Sam's bed was piled high with dirty clothes. Nancy wondered how he could sleep on it.

Laura picked up a pair of old black high-tops.

"These are the ones he wears every

day," she said. "Except today he's wearing sandals."

Nancy looked at the shoes. They had black laces.

"Where are his in-line skates?" Nancy asked Laura.

"In the closet," Laura said.

She pointed to a large walk-in closet on the far side of the room.

"Can we?" Nancy asked, staring at the closet door.

"Sure," Laura said.

Nancy and Laura opened the closet door and stepped inside.

"Here they are," Laura said, lifting one of the heavy skates. "But they're blue. With green-and-blue laces."

Nancy nodded. Then she knelt down to look at a row of shoes that were lined up along the back wall of the closet.

One pair of brown loafers—no laces.

One pair of white high-tops—white laces.

One pair of old, torn green basketball shoes—with dirty green laces.

And one pair of gray leather running shoes—with bright blue laces.

"No luck," Nancy said, glancing up at Laura. "Does he have any other shoes?"

"No," Laura said. "Except his football cleats. And they're all black. The laces are black, too."

"Okay. Let's go," Nancy said.

But before Laura could move out of the closet, the door suddenly slammed shut with a bang.

"Hey, let us out!" Laura cried. She pushed on the door with all her might. But it wouldn't move.

They were trapped!

# 7

# Caught in the Closet

Help! Help!" Laura screamed. She pounded on the closet door, but it wouldn't open.

Nancy stumbled to the door, tripping over Sam's shoes. She tried to push the door open, too.

"I can't turn the knob," Nancy cried. "It's stuck!"

Nancy and Laura pounded on the door as hard as they could. But it didn't budge.

Then all at once, Nancy and Laura heard a mean-sounding laugh coming from the other side of the door.

"Ha ha ha, you little brats!" Sam's voice said. "Serves you right for snooping in my room. I'll *never* let you out!"

"Open the door, Sam," Laura shouted. "Right now!"

"No way," Sam snapped. "You're trapped! Forever!"

"I mean it, Sam. Open up or I'll tell Mom!" Laura said.

The room was silent for a moment. Then the door jerked open. Sam stood there in a pair of tan shorts, a sweaty T-shirt, and his sandals.

"Oh, yeah?" he said. "Well, I'll tell Mom that you were spying on my stuff and snooping in my room! Now get out of here, you little twerps."

"Don't be mad at Laura," Nancy said. "It's my fault. I'm trying to find out who's been stealing food around here."

"So?" Sam said.

"So, I saw you take a cookie in the park yesterday," Nancy said.

"So?" Sam said. "I knew one of those kids at the picnic. He's in my math class.

We always take each other's cookies at lunch. It's a joke between us."

"Oh," Nancy said. She cleared her throat. "But how about last night? Did you climb the fence into the Tangs' yard and steal some food from them, too?"

Sam laughed his nasty-sounding laugh. "I wasn't even home last night," he said. "I was at the movies with a bunch of friends."

"Oh," Nancy said again, blushing.

"Get out of here, Laura," Sam said, grabbing his sister by the arm. "You too, Detective Drew."

Nancy and Laura were silent until they were back outside.

Then Nancy let out a sigh of relief. "Sorry if I got you into trouble."

"Don't worry about it," Laura said. "That was fun! I love sneaking around—especially in *his* room. Want any more help?"

"No thanks," Nancy said. "Not right now. I've got to take my dog home."

"Okay," Laura said. "But come back

later and we can snoop around some more."

As soon as Nancy picked up the leash, her puppy started jumping and pulling. She wagged her tail as if to say, "Come on! Let's get out of here!"

Nancy walked to the end of Laura's driveway. The puppy pulled to the left.

"That's not the way home, silly dog," Nancy said.

But the puppy kept pulling to the left. Finally Nancy gave in.

"Okay," she said to her puppy. "We'll take the long way home. We'll go all the way around the block."

Why not? Nancy thought. Her puppy probably wanted to sniff everything. That's how dogs learned their way around a new place.

Nancy walked a short way down the block. Then she saw Kenny Bruder in his front yard.

As soon as he saw Nancy, he called, "Hey, Drew, can I pet your dog? Can I teach her some tricks?" He came running toward Nancy.

"No tricks yet," Nancy said. She pulled her dog back, so that Kenny wouldn't scare her.

Kenny bent down and started to pet the chocolate Lab right away. The puppy licked Kenny's face. Then she began biting Kenny's shoe.

"Hey," Kenny said. "She's chewing my shoe. Make her stop."

Nancy started to pull back on the leash. But all of a sudden, she saw something. She saw what the puppy was chewing on. Nancy's heart started to beat fast.

"Pull her away," Kenny said. "She's chewing up my shoelaces!"

"I know," Nancy said, staring right into Kenny's eyes. "She's chewing your shoelaces. And they don't match!"

# 8

# Sniffing Out the Truth

One of your shoelaces is brand-new, and plain white," Nancy said. "The other one is old, and it's black- and white-striped."

Kenny pulled his foot away from the puppy. His shoelace came untied.

"So what?" Kenny asked, bending down to retie it. "My shoelace broke."

"I know," Nancy said. "And I know *where* it broke, too. At my house— when you were stealing chocolate chip muffins!"

"I didn't," Kenny said quickly. "I

58

don't even eat chocolate. I'm allergic to it."

That's true, Nancy thought. But if he didn't steal the muffins, how did his shoelace get stuck in our screen door?

"I have proof," she said to Kenny. "Right here in my pocket." Nancy pulled out the torn piece of shoelace.

"See?" Nancy said. "It matches one of your laces exactly. This proves you were in our kitchen on Friday."

"Uh . . . well, I was," Kenny said. "But only because I thought I heard someone call my name. I opened the door, but no one was there. So I left."

Nancy didn't believe him. But before she could say anything, the puppy tugged on the leash and broke free.

"Stop! Come back!" Nancy called. She chased the puppy around the house and into Kenny's backyard.

Kenny followed Nancy.

The puppy ran straight to a toolshed in the backyard. She jumped on the shed door, barking and scratching to get in.

"Don't go in there!" Kenny yelled.

Nancy followed her dog up to the shed and put her hand on the door handle.

"Don't! Don't open it!" Kenny shouted.

"Why not?" Nancy said, turning to stare at Kenny.

Kenny didn't answer. What's he trying to hide? Nancy wondered.

Before Kenny could stop her, Nancy yanked the shed door open.

Eagerly, her puppy dashed inside. Then Nancy saw what the puppy was sniffing.

A brown paper bag. A bag of groceries!

"Mrs. Ratazchek's groceries! I knew it!" Nancy said. "The minute I saw your shoelaces, I knew you were the thief!"

Nancy whirled around and put her hands on her hips. She glared at Kenny, who hung his head.

"Yeah," Kenny said. "Okay. I took

the chocolate chip muffins. And those groceries from Mrs. Ratazchek's car."

"And the hamburgers from Mr. Tang's backyard?" Nancy asked.

She glanced to the right, toward Laura McCorry's house. Laura's house was only a few doors away. Dave Tang lived right behind Laura. Kenny could get there easily.

"Yes," Kenny admitted. "I took the hamburgers, too. But how did you know about that?"

"Never mind," Nancy said. But she couldn't help smiling to herself. She felt pretty proud. She knew about everything he'd done.

Or did she?

"Is that all?" Nancy asked. "Is that *all* the food you stole?"

"Yes, honest," Kenny said. He stared at his feet, then looked at Nancy with pleading eyes. "Please don't tell," he said. "Please?"

"Why did you do it?" Nancy asked.

"It wasn't for me," Kenny said. "It was for my dog."

"*Your* dog?" Nancy asked. "But you don't have a dog."

"Well, he's really a stray," Kenny said. "I call him Butch. I fed him, so he would stay."

"Oh," Nancy said, nodding. She knew which dog Kenny meant—the tan stray.

"Butch was following me the other day, when Mrs. Ratazchek came home," Kenny went on. "She went in the house. While she was gone, I took the bag of groceries."

"That's why there were dog footprints on the driveway," Nancy muttered to herself. "Butch was with you."

"Huh?" Kenny asked.

"Never mind," Nancy said. Then she glanced at the bag of groceries in the shed. "But the bag is still full," she said.

"Full of paper stuff," Kenny said. "Napkins and paper plates and stuff like that. And one box of macaroni. The only food in there was a package of hamburger meat."

Nancy looked more closely and saw that Kenny was right. There were a lot of paper goods. But the bag also had a dark red stain from the meat juices.

"That's what my dog smelled," Nancy suddenly realized. She bent down and gave her puppy a hug. "Good dog," Nancy said. "Good job, sniffing out the clues."

The puppy wagged her tail and licked Nancy on the nose.

"I fed the meat to Butch the other day," Kenny said. "But then I ran out of stuff. So when I saw those muffins at your house, I took them."

"Well, you shouldn't have. Chocolate is bad for dogs." Nancy thought for a moment. Then she said, "And then last night you stole the four hamburgers."

Kenny nodded. "Please don't tell," he said again. "I want to keep Butch so badly. And it's working. He stays with me all the time now."

Nancy looked around the yard.

"Where is he now?" she asked.

"I locked him up in the garage when

I saw you coming," Kenny said. "Are you going to tell my mom?"

Suddenly Nancy heard a screen door bang on the back of Kenny's house.

"She doesn't have to tell," Mrs. Bruder said as she came out the door. "I just overheard everything you said."

"Oh, no," Kenny said. He smacked his head with his hands.

Mrs. Bruder came over to Kenny. She bent down and put her arm around him.

"Kenny," she said, "I'm very sorry and upset to hear that you've been stealing food."

"But, Mom—" Kenny started to say.

"No, let me finish," Mrs. Bruder said. "I'm also very sorry that I didn't understand how much you wanted a dog."

Kenny looked at his mom. "I'm sorry I took the food," he said. "But I really like Butch. And he likes me."

"Well," Mrs. Bruder said. "The first thing we need to do is return all these groceries to Mrs. Ratazchek. And you'll tell her you're sorry."

Kenny nodded again.

"I'll give you some money to pay for the hamburger," Mrs. Bruder went on. "And then you need to apologize to Hannah Gruen about the muffins. And to Mr. Tang."

"Okay," Kenny said quietly.

He started to pick up the bag of groceries from the shed. But his mother stopped him.

"Wait a minute," she said. "First you'd better let Butch out of the garage. I'd like to meet this dog—since he's going to be living with us from now on."

Kenny's face lit up. "Really? You mean it? We can keep him?" he cried.

"Yes," his mother said. "If no one claims him. Of course, we'll have to take him to the vet, to get him some shots."

Kenny made a face. "Yuck. I hate shots," he said.

Nancy laughed. "Don't worry," she said, smiling. "Dogs don't mind too much."

Nancy picked up her puppy's leash.

"Well, I'd better go," Nancy said.

"Thank you, Nancy," Mrs. Bruder said. "You've been a big help."

Nancy smiled. She was glad she had solved the mystery—and helped Kenny get a dog.

But mostly she was glad that she could prove to Hannah that her puppy hadn't eaten those muffins after all.

Nancy ran home and burst in through the kitchen door.

"Guess what?" she said to Hannah and her father. "I caught the muffin thief!" Nancy quickly told them the whole story.

"Well, that explains it," Hannah said. "See? I *knew* your puppy wasn't guilty after all!"

Nancy and her father laughed. Then the puppy ran up to Hannah and started wagging her tail.

Hannah bent down to pet her.

"You wouldn't eat my chocolate chip muffins," Hannah cooed to the puppy. "No, you wouldn't. You're not a chocolate chipster—even if you *are* a chocolate Lab."

"That's it!" Nancy cried.

"What?" Hannah asked.

"Her name," Nancy said. "Chocolate Chip! And we can call her Chip for short. Come here, Chocolate Chip. Come here, Chip."

Instantly the puppy ran to Nancy, wagging her tail.

"See? She likes that name," Nancy said, beaming.

She picked up the puppy and cuddled her in her arms, hugging her tight.

"Chip, you're the best dog in the whole world," Nancy said. "And thank you, Hannah. You thought of the perfect name."

Then Nancy put her puppy back in her crate so she could rest. It had been a big morning. The puppy seemed tired.

Besides, there was something important Nancy wanted to do.

She ran up to her room and took out her special blue notebook. She opened it to the next clean page.

Then she wrote:

This weekend I got a new puppy
and solved the Mystery of the
Missing Muffins. I also found out
how it feels to be accused of
something you didn't do.

Guess what? It doesn't feel good.

From now on, I'm going to think
really hard before I accuse anyone
of anything. (Especially Ralph
Caruso!)

P.S. My puppy helped me sniff out
the clues. She's the best dog in the
whole world. I bet she'll help me lots
more when she grows up!

Case closed.

# COBBLE•STREET
## has never been this much fun!

**Join Lily, Tess, and Rosie on their adventures from Newbery Medalist Cynthia Rylant:**

*The Cobble Street Cousins:*
*In Aunt Lucy's Kitchen*
0-689-81708-8

*The Cobble Street Cousins:*
*Special Gifts*
0-689-81715-0

*The Cobble Street Cousins:*
*Summer Party*
0-689-83417-9

*The Cobble Street Cousins:*
*A Little Shopping*
0-689-81709-6

*The Cobble Street Cousins:*
*Some Good News*
0-689-81712-6

*The Cobble Street Cousins:*
*Wedding Flowers*
0-689-83418-7

Aladdin Paperbacks • Simon & Schuster Children's Publishing
www.SimonSaysKids.com

She's sharp.

She's smart.

She's confident.

She's unstoppable.

And she's on your trail.

# THE
# NANCY DREW
# NOTEBOOKS®

## Do you know a younger Nancy Drew fan?

### Now there are mysteries just for them!